RATS ARE GOOD PETS, TOO

Written by
KATIE LONGUA

Illustrated by
ELLEN T. CRENSHAW

Colors by WHITNEY COGAR

epic!

ANIMAL RESCUE FRIENDS

LEARNING NEW TRICKS

Written by
GILLIAN GOERZ • NORM HARPER • MEGAN KEARNEY •
KATIE LONGUA • BRIAN McLACHLAN • LEONIE O'MOORE •
BARBARA PEREZ MARQUEZ • DIANA PETERFREUND

Illustrated by
SHADIA AMIN • KASIA BABIS •
ELLEN T. CRENSHAW • MATT KAUFENBERG •
MAIKE PLENZKE • LEO TRINIDAD • CHELSEA TROUSDALE

Colors by
WHITNEY COGAR

Edited by
STEPHANIE COOKE • HARRIET LOW

Andrews McMeel
PUBLISHING®

Animal Rescue Friends created by Meika Hashimoto,
Gina Loveless, and Genevieve Kote

Andrews McMeel Publishing
a division of Andrews McMeel Universal
1130 Walnut Street, Kansas City, Missouri 64106

www.andrewsmcmeel.com

Epic! Creations, Inc.
702 Marshall Street, Suite 280
Redwood City, California 94063

www.getepic.com

23 24 25 26 27 VEP 10 9 8 7 6 5 4 3 2

Paperback ISBN: 978-1-5248-8234-1
Hardcover ISBN: 978-1-5248-8235-8

Library of Congress Control Number: 2023934324

Design by Christina Gaugler and Carolyn Bahar
Colors by Whitney Cogar

Made by:
Versa Press
Address and location of manufacturer:
1465 Spring Bay Road,
East Peoria, IL 61611
2nd Printing – 8/04/23

Bell! We just got a new rescue. Could you come help her get settled?

Sure, Fred!

Someone dropped off this rat they found. Can you set up a rodent enclosure?

Sure, but shouldn't we just release it in the field?

Oh no, this is a domestic rat. You can tell by her size and coat color.
Not to mention her charming personality!
SCRITCH

Will you be okay handling this, Bell? I have a busy day today, but I don't mind helping.

I'll be fine!
?

Okay, you can do this. You *love* animals!
YUM
RATCARE

Rats are pets, too.
I *can* do this!

YUM

Phew! There--
that's taken care of.
SHUT!

Huh?

What's wrong?
Are you hungry?
UM

Ick!
FOOD

Sigh
UM

You're supposed to have quite the sense of smell--even better than dogs!
Maybe a fresh scent will help?
Ugh! What's *wrong* with you?

CRACKERS
Okay, the book says rats *love* exercise. Surely *this* will cheer you up!
RAT CARE
Yes!
RAT CARE

CATCH!

Oh! You're so... soft.

And even a little bit cute?

Oh! How did it get so late?

I've got to go now, but I'll be back tomorrow!

The next day.
I see you've made a new friend.
Yeah! But I've tried everything, and I can't cheer her up!

Hi, I'm Amelia. A friend told me you'd posted about finding a rat and...

...oh, Whiskers!

I've been searching everywhere! I'm so glad she's safe. Scoots has been sick with worry.
Wow, she definitely recognizes you two!

Whiskers?

When Whiskers went missing, Scoots and I just weren't the same.

Oh yeah! I read that rats are happiest in pairs--just like most humans!

Thank you for taking care of Whiskers.

If you could just fill out this form before you go...
HA HA HA HA

TREATS

Bye, Whiskers! Don't get into any more trouble, okay?

You weren't afraid of Whiskers, were you?
Who, *me?* No way!

A HARD SHELL TO CRACK

Written by
BARBARA PEREZ MARQUEZ

Illustrated by
KASIA BABIS

Colors by **WHITNEY COGAR**

Animal Rescue Friends. Saturday morning.
Hi, Fred! I'm excited to volunteer today.
Thanks for coming in, Mikey! Here's your to-do list.

Bell got here about an hour ago. Let us know if you need help with anything.
Gotcha.

1. Let animals out of their stalls and fill the water trough.
2. Feed the cats.
treats.
¡Aquí vamos!

Chestnut! Daisy!
Señor Wiggles!
¿Dónde están?
?

Hrm...

~~1. Let animals out of their stalls and fill the water trough.~~
2. Feed the cats.
3. Hand out treats.

CAT FOOD

CAT FOOD

FOOD

Sorry, Mikey--
Bell fed the cats first thing this morning. I meant to tell you, but there was a parakeet emergency and it slipped my mind.
THE MEOW IS A LIE
THE CATS HAVE BEEN FED!
CAT FOOD
It's okay. Has she given treats to the dogs yet?

I don't think so.

DOG TREATS

¡Hola, perros!
DOG TREATS

DOG TREATS

Bell! You did everything on my list!
Oh... sorry about that.

I know you can do a lot, but you gotta let me help.
I'm still getting used to sharing tasks and--
BEEP
BEEP

Oh! That's my last to-do item. I have to meet with a family who wants to adopt.

Estamos buscando...

...una mascota para Hector...

Um, one second... I don't...
?

¡Hola! ¿Cómo les podemos ayudar?

Hector quiere una mascota, pero nuestro nuevo apartamento no acepta mascotas que sean peludas. ¿Pueden ayudarnos?

Por supuesto, un momento por favor.

Hmm...
what about
a lizard? Liz is
still with us.

¿Les interesaría
un lagarto como
mascota?

¡Ay no,
no me gustan
sus lenguas!

Okay, no speedy tongues. What about Sergio?

He's great in small spaces.
And he doesn't make any sudden moves.

Sergio es una tortuga, ¿creen que funcionaria para su familia?

Sergio is perfect for their family!
Here's his adoption paperwork.

Can you review it with them? I'll grab a travel tank for Sergio.
Sure!

ARF
¡Gracias!

Thanks for being patient with me. Looks like I have a lot to learn about giving up control and accepting help.
RIIING

You should get that!
RIIING

Animal Rescue Friends, how can we help you today?

CAT
FOOD

NOAH AND CLOVER

Written by
KATIE LONGUA

Illustrated by
CHELSEA TROUSDALE

Colors by **WHITNEY COGAR**

Hi, Noah! I'm glad you're here.
We have a new rescue I'd love for you to meet.

This is Clover.
She's so sweet!

Oh no, what happened?!
Clover recently lost her leg in an accident. But it's okay--most dogs with three legs can live long, happy lives.

She'll need time to adjust, of course, but I have a feeling that you can help Clover get back on her feet.
I guess I could try.

I know you can do it!

There are some tricks you can use to help Clover adjust to tripod life.
Tripod?
It's a word sometimes used to describe a pet with three legs.

She needs to learn to balance and redistribute her weight.
You can hold these handles up to give her some support when you take her out for a walk.

Tuesday.

Wednesday.

Thursday.
Whoa! Having three legs sure doesn't slow you down!

Friday.

Ahhh!

Wow, Clover is doing great!
I think she's ready to meet some people. I'm going to add her to the Animal Rescue Friends adoption page.

She's a quick learner!
She is a really special dog. I'll set up a meet and greet for tomorrow. Can you be there?
Yeah!
WOOF!

Saturday.
Are you ready to meet some people, Clover?
She sure seems like it!

How many visits does she have lined up?
There are four scheduled, but more people might drop in.
Many potential adopters don't show up for their appointments, though.

Four doesn't seem like a lot--

Is Clover ready? We need to get started.

Whoa!

First up is Silvia Smiles!

OMG! I'm at ARF and about to meet the *cutest* dog. #AdoptDontShop!

Isn't she *so* amazing?
Um, do you want to fill out an application to adopt Clover?
REC

Oh no, I'm just filming a rescue pet awareness series, and Clover seems like the perfect costar!
Okay, so that's a *no.*

We'd love a dog to help us get out for more walks--
Oh my, that's a little *too much* energy!

I would love to adopt a dog, but they'd have to get along with Mittens.
HISSSSS!

I love dogs, but I...I--

I think I might be allergic.
ACHOO!

Just one more family left who's interested in Clover...

Wow, they're really getting along!
We saw her on the website and *knew* we had to meet her.
She's so cute!

We don't have any other pets, so Clover will get all our love and attention.

What do *you* think, Clover?

WOOF!

I just know Clover's going to do great with you and your dad! And if she still needs some help with stairs or jumping into the car, you can use her sling.

But you probably won't need it for walks!

DAPHNE AND THE DUCKLINGS

Written by
MEGAN KEARNEY

Illustrated by
MATT KAUFENBERG

Colors by **WHITNEY COGAR**

Good morning, everyone!
ARF
Animal Rescue Friends

Morning, Maddie!
Hey, Noah! Hi, Mikey! Where's Fred?

Right here, but not for long! I have to pick up a few of our rescues from the vet.
WHUFF!

Aww! Who's this?

Everyone, meet Daphne.
Oh, she's a border collie! They're herding dogs, right?
That's right!
TROT!
TROT! TROT!

But why is she here? She has a collar and tags.
WHUFF!

Daphne wandered away from the farm down the road. Her people can't pick her up until this afternoon, so she's our guest for now.

Border collies need lots of stimulation, which is why they're such good working dogs.
Maybe one of you could take her with you on your rounds?
TROT! TROT! TROT!

I don't mind taking her!
Besides, she's already taking *me!* Ha ha!
WHUFF!

Great! Daphne, be a good helper.
WHUFF!

Oh, and one more bit of news--our ducklings started hatching last night!
Ducklings!

And right on schedule.
Their mama's wing is all patched up, and she comes back from the vet today.

Bell is already in the barn with the ducklings. Noah, you're helping out there today. Maddie and Mikey, you can go visit them after your chores are done, if you'd like.

I can't wait to finish up so I can see the ducklings!
I bet they're really cute!

You have a cool assistant, Maddie. I bet you'll get through your chores lightning fast.

I think you're right, Mikey. I'm gonna get everything done in record time!

ARF
See you at the barn!
Okay!
WHUFF!
Easy, Daphne! I'm coming!

Noah!
Come see the ducklings!

How many are there? Did they all hatch?

They sure did! Most of them hatched last night, but I got to see the final two hatch this morning!
Aw, look at them!
WAK!
WAK!

But wait--
weren't there six eggs?
Huh.
Let's see...

You're right!
One duckling is missing!

Where could it have gone?
Heeeere, lil' duckie...

Little duckie?

Anyone in here?

Any ducklings up here?

I found it!

Thank goodness! Back you go, little buddy.

Hold on--that should make six, but we're a few ducklings short of a flock!
What?

They're smaller than usual, so they're escaping through the wire.
Oh no!
POP!

Their mama will be back from the vet soon. We've got to find them all before then!

Meanwhile...
Okay, work time! Let's see...

Hmm, looks like we're on reptile room and small-animal duty.

In a hurry to get started? I guess you like to be busy!
WHUFF!

Well, that works for me. I want to finish up so I can see the ducklings!

Let's start with the reptile room.
WHUFF!

Whoa! Whoooa!

CRASH

Daphne, I know your job usually includes keeping sheep where they need to be...
...but let's save that energy for the rest of our chores!
WHUFF?

Back in the barn...
PANT
I think that's all of them.
How can anything with webbed feet run so fast?

All this clutter is a hazard. But how else can we keep them in their pen?

Oh no, you don't!

Gotcha!
Nice try, my fine feathered--

WAK!
--friend?

Verrry funny!

How do ducks keep track of their ducklings?
Babies usually imprint on their mother and follow her around, right?

Yeah, but these guys hatched in an ***incubator!*** They haven't even seen their mom yet!
And she won't arrive until later today. Hmmm...

We're going to need a full-time duck nanny until she gets here!

Meanwhile, in the reptile room...

Okay--first up, I need to check the temperature and humidity in each terrarium.

Are you toasty enough?

Just a quick spritz for you, Karmen.

Snack time!
MEAL WORM

Don't worry--you and I can have something less wriggly for ***our*** snack, Daphne.
WHINE
MEAL WORM

REPTILES
SMALL ANIMALS
This is one of my favorite rooms.

?

Hi, Harrison!

WHUFF! WHUFF! WHUFF!

WHUFF!

What is it, Daphne?

WHOOP!

WHOOP!

WHOOP!

Aw, I know you want to help, but the guinea pigs don't need rounding up. They're already where they need to be.
WHINE
WHOOP!

WHOOP!

Hey! I don't need rounding up, either!
Where are we going?
WHUFF!

We're not done with our jobs yet!
Hi, Maddie. I just finished up. Do you want to go to the barn to see--

FWIP!

WHUFF!
Daphne, no--

NYROOOM!

ARF
Daphne!

Come back, girl!
Look! She's going into the barn.

WHOOOSH!

WHUFF!

We're so sorry!
She just got away!

ZIP!

ZIP!

ZIP!

WHUFF!
WAK!

CLICK!

Daphne, you're a genius! You saved us from a duckling disaster!
WHUFF!

One... two...three...

Daphne should be out here with the volunteers.

I hope she wasn't too much trouble!

Oh good! You found a job to keep her busy!

WAK!

WHUFF!

Daphne, you troublemaker, running off and bothering these nice folks!
Thanks for watching her until we could get here. I know she can be a real handful!

Well, she definitely likes to be busy.
But she wound up being a ***huge*** help!

Uh-oh!
WAK!

WHUFF!
WAK!
WAK!
WAK!

Looks like Daphne made some friends today!
WAK!
WAK!

We're really glad their mama is back. It was a challenge keeping these ducks, er... in a row.
We couldn't have done it without Daphne.

WHIIIINE

You know, Carol, that old chicken coop down by the pond is empty...
It would be ***so cute*** to have a family of ducks living there!
Mariko, I was just thinking the same thing!

If Daphne loves them, we love them, too. Are they up for adoption, Fred?
Absolutely! Now that Mama is better, they're all available. Let's head to the office to fill out an application.

Aw, I love a happy ending!
Just one problem--there are only five ducklings. One is missing!

What do you think, Daphne? Can you help us one last time?
WHUFF!

WAK!

Written by
BRIAN McLACHLAN

Illustrated by
LEO TRINIDAD

Colors by **WHITNEY COGAR**

Animal Rescue Friends.
Saturday morning.

Help! You've gotta help! Major Sprinkles is missing!
BANG!

Major Sprinkles?
He's my pet beagle. He's been missing since last night.

How did he get lost?
We were walking when a storm came out of nowhere. The thunder scared him, and he ran off. I looked everywhere, but I couldn't find him. I don't know what to do.
It's going to be okay. We'll find him!

There's a chance that Major Sprinkles is still nearby. I'll make some missing posters, and we'll post them around the park. Can you email me his picture?
Done.

Good. Now, there's also a chance he knows his way home. Did you leave out food and some of your clothes so he can catch your scent?
No, but I'll text my dad to do that.

Great. These are ready.
Missing
Rescue Friends
Wow, that was fast!

I'm Noah, by the way.
Hu.
Let's go find your dog!

Here, boy!
Major Sprinkles!

Missing
Contact Animal Rescue Friends
This is where he ran off.

Have you seen my dog?

Nope.
He's missing? That's terrible!
Sorry, I haven't seen him.

Marwyn ran away a few months ago. It was awful not knowing where she was.

I'm really sorry your dog is missing. It's a scary feeling.
Yeah. It really is.

I'm glad you found your dog, though.
Me too. Good luck finding Major Sprinkles!

Just finished hanging up a few posters. Where else does your dog like to play?
Well, there's the big fountain that he likes to splash around in.
Even though he's not supposed to.

Let's go!
Missing
Contact Animal Rescue Friends

CARICATURES

NOT DOGS

I haven't seen him, but if you give me one of these posters, I'll ask the other dog walkers to keep an eye out.
Contact Animal Rescue Friends
Thanks, Maddie!

Major Sprinkles! Major Sprinkles!

He's not here.
It's like looking for a needle in a haystack.

Don't give up--we'll find him. But I think we could use a little break.

Just Chillin'
Just Chillin'
Want some ice cream?
I guess I could go for some chocolate ice cream.

I hope we find Major Sprinkles soon.
Major sprinkles? I have major sprinkles! Rainbow sprinkles, chocolate sprinkles--

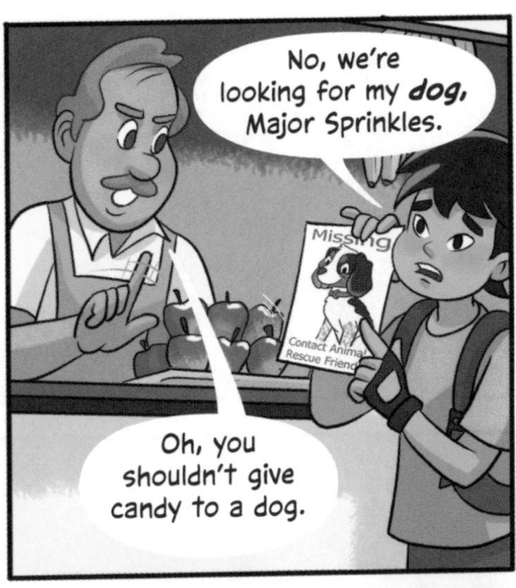
No, we're looking for my *dog*, Major Sprinkles.
Missing
Contact Animal Rescue Friends
Oh, you shouldn't give candy to a dog.

You should give them fresh fruit. It's much healthier!
We have bananas, strawberries, blueberries--

Wait-- that's it!

My family and I go berry picking every Sunday at a farm nearby.
Major Sprinkles has so much fun with the dogs there. And he *loves* eating blueberries.
Let's check there next!

YOU'LL DIG
OUR BERRIED
TREASURE
Major Sprinkles?

Major Sprinkles!

I'm so happy
we found you!

I missed
you, boy.

We didn't find a
needle in a haystack--
we found a ***beagle*** in
a haystack!
ARF!

CHATTY BIRD

Written by
LEONIE O'MOORE

Illustrated by
SHADIA AMIN

Colors by **WHITNEY COGAR**

It's a busy day today. We've got to feed all the animals, take the dogs on walks, and clean the snakes' tanks!
AWK!
More crackers.

You're very chatty, aren't you?

You're very chatty, aren't you?

Hey! That's a good trick. You sound just like me!

CLICK!

There we go. Now you're on our social pages, and hopefully your family will see your picture.

Oh, I forgot to post this video of me giving the cats belly rubs. Can't believe they let me!

Meeow.
Meeow.

Uh-oh. Sounds like a cat got loose.

Here, kitty kitty...
awk
awk

Sorry I'm a little late, Fred!

Give cats belly rub!

Give cats belly rub!
Okay, okay, Fred, I'll add it to my list.

A little later.
Hi!
Hi, Fred! We got too much hay for Hopper, so I thought I'd share the extra.

Can I help with anything else?

Take snakes for walk!

Uhh... okay, Fred.

Meanwhile...

I don't understand why Fred told me to do this.

Maybe I should go ask him.

Fred, are you in here?
Bring crackers, please.

Oh, hello. When did you get here?
awk awk

I brought these crackers for Fred, but I'm sure he won't mind sharing.
Anyway, I'm Bell. Can you talk? I know some parrots can.
awk

See you later. I wonder where Fred is...

Hi, Mikey. Have you seen--

What are you *doing?!*

I'm getting the snakes ready for their walk. Do we have any smaller collars?

That doesn't make sense.
But, uh... Fred told me to do it.

Why are you wearing shredded oven mitts?

Come on. We're going to find Fred and get this all sorted out.

Hi, you two. You know, I could've sworn I heard a loose cat, but I can't find one.
By the way, have you met our new greeter?

Fred, why do you keep telling us to do strange chores? It isn't April Fools' Day!

What strange chores? I haven't added anything new to your lists.

Meeow.
Meeow.
There was no loose cat--it was *you!*

That's amazing!
Ah, of course--his impressions!
So *he* was the one giving us chores?
He must have heard me reading the chores lists earlier, and then mimicked them!

But why was he trying to trick us?
He wasn't. Cockatoos imitate sounds made by their flock. For pet cockatoos, their flocks are humans--and in this case, probably a cat, too.

Bring crackers, please.
You're not Fred!
I *am* Fred.

Oh, thank goodness! You found my bird.
Hello! Time to go home.
AWK! AWK!

I hope he hasn't been too much trouble. He likes to cause mischief.

He tricked my houseguest into opening a window. That's how he got out.

Come on, Fred--let's go home.

He really *is* Fred!

AMARA, OPIE, AND ALMA
Written by
GILLIAN GOERZ
Illustrated by
SHADIA AMIN
Colors by WHITNEY COGAR

I won't be gone long, Bell, but there's a chance the new volunteer will arrive before I get back.
CLACK
CLACK

If she does, show her around. You know what to do!
Sure, Fred! What's her--

CLICK!
--name?

CLACKITY
CLACK
CLACK

WHOOSH
Hi, you must be--

Amara. From Art Club. Here to volunteer.
Sorry! What's that?

Okay, let's get started. You can leave your bag behind the counter and come with me.
Oh no, I need to keep this with me.
Suit yourself. This way.

...and this is the small-rescues room. Tasks here include cleaning out enclosures, making sure the water is--
Can I see the kittens now?

We'll get to them in a minute.
But first I need to teach you how to handle small reptiles, like turtles, geckos--
I'm actually *only* interested in the kittens.

All the animals need attention, Amara. You can't just cut to the fun part.
Of course they all need attention, but *I* am only here for the kittens. Can I see them *now?*

You can't pick and choose! *I* learned how to care for every animal here. It wasn't easy and it took time, but now I'm proud to be able to--

There you are, my beauties!
Hey!

We're not at this part of the tour yet!

What are
you *doing?*

Ooooh!

I'm just *obsessed*
with cats right now.
They move in this liquid
way--smooth, like water.
Wow!
You're really
good.

You know,
you're right.
Cats *do* move
like liquid.
I never
noticed that
before.

It would
be great to
get closer.
Can I go
in?
Okay, but only for a minute.
This mother and her kittens
were brought in recently, and
they're pretty rambunctious.
Watch out for *Alma* and
Opie, especially.

How do you draw them when they're moving so much?
It can be tough! Instead of getting the details exactly right, I try to capture their energy. I might just draw lines, shapes...

...this kind of thing.
Wow.

Last week I couldn't get ***enough*** of horses. But I had to draw all of these from photos.
You know we have horses here, right?

You do?!
Totally! We'll get to them if I can just finish the tour--

Eeee!
Ahhh!
YOOOOWL
CLANK
EEEEEE
OW, ALMA!
HH/////SSSS
OPIE, NO!

HA HA HA HA HA HA HA HA HA HA

I'm back!
Bell? Hello?

Bell, Amara!
Are you okay?
I think so...
Oh no!

Your sketchbook!

It's...

...a work of *art!*

It's my first human-animal collaboration! This captures cat energy on a whole new level.
Hello?

Um, hi. I'm Junie, and I'm here to volunteer?
Hi, Junie! You're just in time to see how colorful volunteering can be!

You're not the volunteer?
Amara comes in to draw the animals every few weeks. I guess it's always happened on your days off.
Junie, I'll take you to the front desk. We can get started while these two clean up.

I'm really sorry I was so pushy before. I misunderstood why you were here.
Yeah, I can be a little pushy myself.
It's cool you volunteer here. You must really know your stuff.

Thanks. I love animals.
They're the best!

Can I still come back? Even though...this happened?
Totally! Things get messy here all the time. Wait until you see the horses!

The horses! Can we see them ***now?***

After we clean this up, of course. Then I'd love the tour.

PUUUURRRRR
PUUURRRR

BEES!

Written by
LEONIE O'MOORE

Illustrated by
ELLEN T. CRENSHAW

Colors by **WHITNEY COGAR**

Hey, Maddie! There were leftovers from the school bake sale today. I saved you a triple-chocolate cupcake.
Yum, my favorite!
Arrghhh!
BZZZ BZZZ
A wasp!
BZZZ BZZZ
The cupcakes!

It's just a little bee!
BZZZ BZZZ

Sorry I dropped the cupcakes. I'm kinda scared of wasps and bees.

It's okay.
Look! That bee is flying to the others by the barn.

You stay here. I'll go check it out.

BZZZ
BZZZ

I found a nest. We should tell Fred.

Wow! That's so exciting!

How do we get rid of them?

Bees are an endangered species. I know you're scared, but we need to help them.

Are you calling an exterminator?
I'm calling a beekeeper.

Two hours later.

ARF

Animal Rescue Friends

This is Suzie, a local beekeeper. She's going to help us move the bees.
Hi!

Should we all be wearing suits? Will we get stung?

Well, female bees *can* sting, but only if they feel threatened.
If you stand back a few feet, they'll leave you alone.

I'll move the bees from the nest to this box hive, and then I can safely transport them to my apiary.
BZZZZZ
Nest, hive, apiary--what's the difference?

A home that bees make for themselves, like the one hanging from the barn, is called a *nest.*

A home that people make for them, like the one I brought, is called a *hive.*

And the place where we keep the hives is called an *apiary.*

Bell, can you hold this for me? The smoke helps calm the bees.
If they come near you, just give it a squirt.
I'm taking some of the honeycomb out. I've managed to find the queen.
BZZZ BZZZ
BZZZZ
The worker bees will follow the queen here to the hive.
What sort of work do they do?
They have lots of jobs...

...like building the comb, cleaning, scouting for food...
Bzzz Bzzzz

...and guarding the hive from wasps.
Bzzzzzz
See, Bell? Bees don't like wasps, either!

These cells hold the bees' brood, as well as plant nectar that eventually turns into honey.

The workers also pollinate plants, giving us lots of beautiful flowers and yummy fruit.
The honey's my favorite part!

Wow. They do a lot more than I thought.
They're very busy bees!
Just like you, Bell!

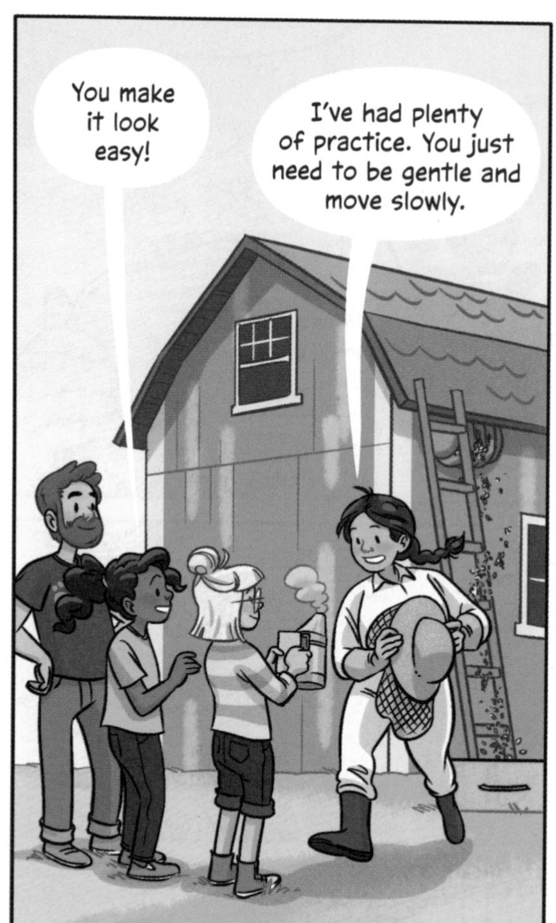
You make it look easy!
I've had plenty of practice. You just need to be gentle and move slowly.

Bzzzz
Bzzzzz
Bzzzzzz

I like to name the queen in each of my colonies. Maddie, since you found the nest, would you like to name this one?

Well, Bell saw the first bee. I think she should name it.

How about Cupcake?
Queen Cupcake. I love that!

Bees aren't as scary as I thought. I'd like to learn more about them.

When I was your age, I loved gardening with my grandma, and I was really curious about all the bees buzzing around.

This book answered a lot of my questions.
BEE FACTS

Thanks!
BEE FACTS

Come visit Queen Cupcake and her hive anytime.

The next day.
Mmmm! Do I smell honey buns?
Thanks, Bell. What's the occasion?

Just to say thanks. You were both right--bees are important, and they're not so scary once you learn about them.

Did you know that bees and butterflies pollinate 75 percent of the world's flowering plants? And that the workers are all female?
And that honeybees communicate by doing a little dance? And that if you see a tired bee, you can feed it sugar water to give it energy?

They're actually quite ***bee***utiful.
ha ha ha
They sure are, Bell. They sure are.

BZZZ BZZZ

HOUDINI AT HOME

Written by
DIANA PETERFREUND

Illustrated by
MAIKE PLENZKE

Colors by **WHITNEY COGAR**

Morning, Houdini! How was your first night?
Don't worry. Today I'll build your enclosure, and you can get out of that...

...cage?

Heeeeeeeere, Houdini.

You little escape artist!

You'll have plenty of room to explore in your new enclosure.
Just behave while I set it up!

Now, where did I put those instructions?

Rabbi
Care
Instructio

!!!

What did they say again?
Enclosure panels, floor mat, hay, litter tray...

Hmm. Do I cover the floor mat with hay?
Or is the hay meant to be food?
HAY

I bet I can find some instructions online.

Why won't it turn on?

Oh no!

Houdini!

Mom's going to flip...

Ugh!

You won't get away this time!

Gotcha!

Uh-oh...

CRASH

We sure caused a lot of trouble.

KNOCK
KNOCK
What's going on in there?!
I heard a crash.

Oh no--it's Mr. Lutz, the landlord!

What will he say about this mess?

You'd better not be hiding another dog--
KNOCK
KNOCK
It's not a dog! Mom checked, and the lease says we can have a rabbit.

A rabbit?

I love rabbits!

That was my first bunny, Angel...

...and these spotted guys are Belly and Button...

SPRING

Sorry-- he's a bit of a handful.
Rabbits can be tricky to care for!
I've been trying to build an enclosure for him, but he ate the instructions.

Let me help you rabbit-proof.
It'll be safer for Houdini *and* the apartment.

A strip of masking tape here will keep him from chewing.

Rabbits *love* electrical cords, so hide them away!

Houdini wants to explore.
We just need to build him a safe place to do it.

Thanks so much for all your help, Mr. Lutz.

No problem! Now all we need is Houdini.

DRAKE AND ODIN

Written by
NORM HARPER

Illustrated by
CHELSEA TROUSDALE

Colors by **WHITNEY COGAR**

ARF
ADOPTION DAY

Wow.
There are a lot of people here...

You can wear it if you want to, Drake. But don't dawdle, okay?
Okay!

Evildoers, beware...

...Crimson Canine has arrived!

C'mon, let's go find you a sidekick.

Welcome to Animal Rescue Friends. What can we help you with today?
I seek your bravest warrior!

As you can see, Drake--sorry, *Crimson Canine*--can be pretty bold when he's wearing his mask.
We're hoping to find a companion who will help him feel just as confident when he's using his *secret identity.*

A brave companion, huh? If it's okay, Fred, I think I know just the dog.
Sure thing, Noah.

I like your cape.
Thanks!

That's Odin, the bravest dog I've ever met.

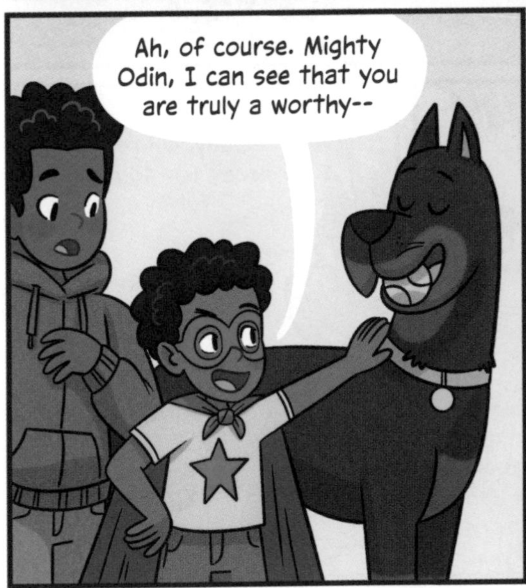
Ah, of course. Mighty Odin, I can see that you are truly a worthy--

Oh, that's not Odin.

This is Odin.
But...

This is a dog built for adventures. What's his name?
That's Anvil. He's big, but... he's not really what I'd call an adventurer.

Take some time to get to know them both a bit. Choosing a sidekick is a big decision.

Okay, who's ready for some fun?

Ha ha!
I've got you now,
Doctor Despot!

You don't
want to be a
villain, huh?

How about
a game of fetch?

Go get it!

Anvil!

Wow, Odin!
ARF! ARF!
ARF!

ARF!

Whoa.

My hero!

Is everything okay?
There was a snake.
But it's gone now.

Grass snakes are pretty common here. They're harmless, but it's still best to leave them alone.
Odin made sure I was safe! He was so brave.

He's the bravest dog I've ever met!

It was good to meet you, Anvil. I hope this helps *you* feel a little braver.

What's this? No more Crimson Canine?
Nah, Anvil needed it more.
I can already tell that Odin is going to teach me a lot about being brave without a mask and cape.

ANIMAL RESCUE FRIENDS

ADOPTION FORM

ANIMAL TYPE:

Dog

ANIMAL BREED:

Mixed breed

ANIMAL'S NAME:

Clover

ANIMAL'S LIKES:

Walks

Chew toys

Belly rubs

ANIMAL'S DISLIKES:

School buses

Pickles

Busy streets

ANIMAL RESCUE FRIENDS
ADOPTION FORM

ANIMAL TYPE:
Dog

ANIMAL BREED:
Poodle mix

ANIMAL'S NAME:
Odin

ANIMAL'S LIKES:
Superheroes
Fetch
Peanut butter

ANIMAL'S DISLIKES:
Snakes
Cats
Being underestimated

ANIMAL RESCUE FRIENDS

ADOPTION FORM

ANIMAL TYPE:
Dog

ANIMAL BREED:
Great dane

ANIMAL'S NAME:
Anvil

ANIMAL'S LIKES:
Fetch
Snuggles
Treats

ANIMAL'S DISLIKES:
Surprises
Snakes
Sudden movements

ANIMAL RESCUE FRIENDS

ADOPTION FORM

ANIMAL TYPE:

Rabbit

ANIMAL BREED:

Dutch

ANIMAL'S NAME:

Houdini

ANIMAL'S LIKES:

Exploring new spaces

Carrots

Chewing

ANIMAL'S DISLIKES:

Cages

Lamps

Cold weather

ANIMAL RESCUE FRIENDS
ADOPTION FORM

ANIMAL TYPE:
Bird

ANIMAL BREED:
Cockatoo

ANIMAL'S NAME:
Fred

ANIMAL'S LIKES:
Crackers
Chatting
Practical jokes

ANIMAL'S DISLIKES:
Being alone
Silence
Boring humans

ANIMAL RESCUE FRIENDS

ADOPTION FORM

ANIMAL TYPE:

Dog

ANIMAL BREED:

Beagle

ANIMAL'S NAME:

Major Sprinkles

ANIMAL'S LIKES:

Blueberries

Splashing in fountains

Other dogs

ANIMAL'S DISLIKES:

Thunder

Storms

Getting lost

ANIMAL RESCUE FRIENDS
ADOPTION FORM

ANIMAL TYPE:
Dog

ANIMAL BREED:
Border collie

ANIMAL'S NAME:
Daphne

ANIMAL'S LIKES:
Ducks
Open fields
Herding

ANIMAL'S DISLIKES:
Sitting still
Boredom
Squirrels

ANIMAL RESCUE FRIENDS

ADOPTION FORM

ANIMAL TYPE:
Cat

ANIMAL BREED:
Mixed breed

ANIMAL'S NAME:
Alma

ANIMAL'S LIKES:
Preening
Jumping
Being painted

ANIMAL'S DISLIKES:
Baths
Being ignored
Closed doors

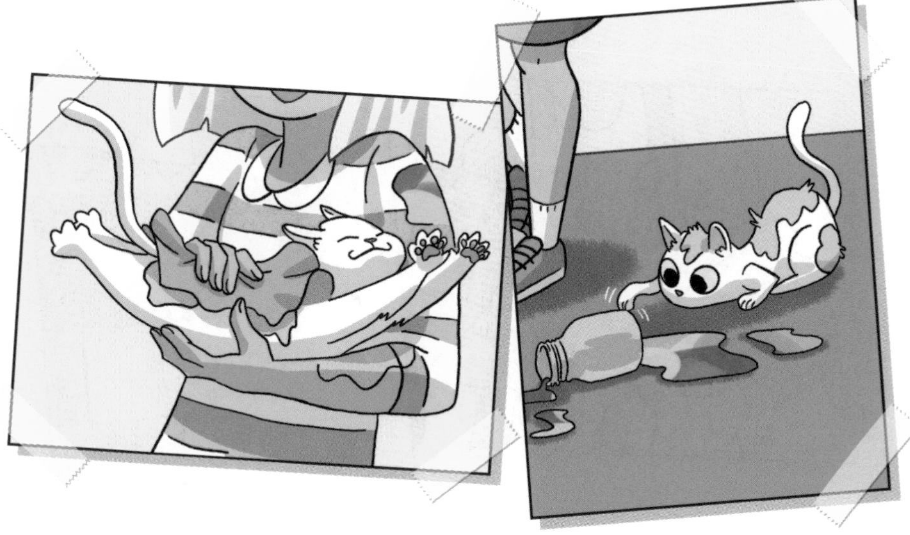

ANIMAL RESCUE FRIENDS

ADOPTION FORM

ANIMAL TYPE:

Cat

ANIMAL BREED:

British shorthair

ANIMAL'S NAME:

Opie

ANIMAL'S LIKES:

Kibble

Long naps

Getting messy

ANIMAL'S DISLIKES:

Dogs

Diet cat food

Loud noises

ANIMAL RESCUE FRIENDS

ADOPTION FORM

ANIMAL TYPE:

Rat

ANIMAL BREED:

Standard rat

ANIMAL'S NAME:

Whiskers

ANIMAL'S LIKES:

Pats

Company

Attention

ANIMAL'S DISLIKES:

Change

Getting wet

Falling

ANIMAL RESCUE FRIENDS

ADOPTION FORM

ANIMAL TYPE:

Turtle

ANIMAL BREED:

Wood turtle

ANIMAL'S NAME:

Sergio

ANIMAL'S LIKES:

His terrarium

Soothing music

Leafy greens

ANIMAL'S DISLIKES:

Moving fast

Moldy lettuce

Being woken up

ANIMAL RESCUE FRIENDS
ADOPTION FORM

ANIMAL TYPE:
Duck

ANIMAL BREED:
American Pekin

ANIMAL'S NAME:
Ducklings 1–6

ANIMAL'S LIKES:
Mama duck
Cheeping
Hiding

ANIMAL'S DISLIKES:
Being quiet
Being crowded
Lining up in a row

ABOUT THE CREATORS

AUTHORS

Gillian Goerz is a cartoonist, graphic recorder, and author. Her graphic novel *Shirley and Jamila Save Their Summer* (Dial) was praised by the *New York Times* and made the CBC's and the New York Public Library's Best Books of the Year lists. Her second book, *Shirley and Jamila's Big Fall*, won the Doug Wright Award for best kids' book. Gillian has a passion for communication and sharing stories through multiple mediums. Visit her online at gilliang.com.

Norm Harper is a Los Angeles–based writer. He likes to tell stories about silly talking animals, scary monsters, and characters learning that the world isn't remotely what they thought it was. He usually manages to fit in all three. His work includes the Eisner-nominated *Rikki* and the Silver Ledger Award–winning YA fantasy *Haphaven*.

Megan Kearney is a writer and cartoonist. She lives in Toronto with her family and a very old gentleman rabbit. She loves ghost stories, garage sales, and a good cup of tea.

Katie Longua is an artist and magical girl. She's been publishing her own comics for over ten years, including the award-winning *RÖK*, *Her Space Opera*, and *Munchies*. She now works mainly as part of Triple Dream Comics, an Eisner-nominated, all-female comic-making team. She lives in a haunted house with her partner, Josh, and a small army of transforming robots.

Brian McLachlan is the cartoonist of the RPG graphic novel *Complete the Quest: The Poisonous Library* and the very practical *Draw Out the Story: 10 Secrets to Creating Your Own Comics*. He writes the monthly *Spruce Street Squad* comic in *Owl Magazine* and lives in Toronto with his family and their very chill cat, Thor.

Leonie O'Moore is an Irish writer and artist. Her published works include *Heavy Metal* magazine, *Joan Jett and the Blackhearts 40x40*, and *ALIENS Artbook*. She has also conducted comic book workshops in schools, museums, and galleries. She developed and wrote the curriculum for the BA degree course Comics and Graphic Novels for Teesside University, UK. She currently resides in sunny California, where she enjoys eating ice cream and looking at the sea.

Barbara Perez Marquez was born and raised in the Dominican Republic and now lives in Baltimore, Maryland. She's part of the team behind the acclaimed Eisner-nominated graphic novel series *The Cardboard Kingdom*. Her next graphic novel, *The Library of Memories* (Little, Brown), cocreated alongside Lissy Marlin, is due out in 2025. You can visit her online at mustachebabs.com.

Diana Peterfreund is the author of fifteen books for children, teens, and adults, as well as dozens of short stories. She lives outside of Washington, DC, with two daughters who live for comic books and two rescue cats who live for scritches. Visit her online at dianapeterfreund.com.

ILLUSTRATORS

Shadia Amin is a Colombian comic artist and illustrator. She enjoys drawing fantasy, action, and the little joys in life, focusing on emotional and dynamic art. Her work includes *Aggretsuko*, *Spider-Ham*, and *Dumb and Dumber*. When she is not working on comics, she is cooking a lot and loving on her dog, cat, and husband.

Kasia Babis is a Polish illustrator, comic artist, and politician also known as Kittypat or Kiciputek. She uses her art to comment on current social or political issues and other everyday events. She is an author of picture books for children and a concept artist in the game industry.

Ellen T. Crenshaw is a cartoonist and illustrator for books, editorial, comics, and children's media. She is the cocreator, with Colleen AF Venable, of *Kiss Number 8*, which was nominated for an Eisner Award and longlisted for a National Book Award. She is also the creator of *What Was the Turning Point of the Civil War?: Alfred Waud Goes to Gettysburg*, a *Who HQ* Graphic Novel. Visit her online at ellencrenshaw.com.

Matt Kaufenberg is a freelance illustrator living in Minnesota with his wife and their five children. His work includes numerous children's books, toy designs, and more. He enjoys spending time with his family and collecting way too many comics and toys.

ILLUSTRATORS

Maike Plenzke is a freelance illustrator from Berlin, Germany. She illustrates books, magazines, and more from a studio filled with plants. When she's not creating art, she loves to walk in the sun or watch movies from her couch with her husband and dog.

Leo Trinidad is an illustrator and storyboard artist from Costa Rica. He has been creating content for children's books and TV shows for fifteen years and has worked on productions for Cartoon Network, Disney, Sony Pictures, and DreamWorks.

Chelsea Trousdale is a character designer and illustrator based in Salt Lake City, Utah, where she lives with her husband and two cats. She is passionate about character design, storytelling, and creating content that is engaging and inspiring. She has created artwork for clients including Waterford Upstart, the Society of Visual Storytelling, Epic Originals, and Atomic Cartoons.

COLORIST

Whitney Cogar is a comic colorist and illustrator from Savannah, Georgia. She contributed colors to the two-time Eisner Award–winning *Giant Days* (Boom! Studios), the Ringo Award–winning *The O.Z.*, the *Steven Universe* comic series (Boom! Studios), and Lucy Knisley's *Peapod Farm* series (Penguin Random House). She enjoys building punchy, rich environments in her work and designing enamel pins.

Stephanie Cooke is an award-nominated writer and editor based in Toronto. When she's not writing, reading, or coming up with cringe-worthy puns, she can be found curled up with her snuggly cat...that she is very allergic to. Her graphic novels, *Oh My Gods!* and *Paranorthern*, are out now. Learn more about her at stephaniecooke.ca.

Harriet Low is a children's and young adult book editor based in Rhode Island. They've edited all sorts of books, from graphic novels to picture books to nonfiction, some of which have even been bestsellers and award-winners. They currently work with talented authors and illustrators on comic series like *Animal Rescue Friends* at Epic. When they aren't editing, they're probably bingeing a webcomic, organizing their stationary, or eating yummy food with friends.